Give Me Wings

Poems selected by
Lee Bennett Hopkins

Illustrated by
Ponder Goembel

Holiday House / New York

Contents

Wake Up, Wings!
Rebecca Kai Dotlich

To see the world
and world-things,
shake awake
those silent
wings.

Speak of soaring;
tell of sky.
Wake up, wings!
Prepare
to fly!

Of Wings
Prince Redcloud

Gazing
at birds
I sing songs
of wings.

Gazing
at sky
I, too,
want
to fly.

I, Icarus
Alden Nowlan

There was a time when I could fly. I swear it.
Perhaps, if I think hard for a moment, I can even tell you the year.
My room was on the ground floor at the rear of the house.
My bed faced a window.
Night after night I lay on my bed and willed myself to fly.
It was hard work, I can tell you.
Sometimes I lay perfectly still for an hour before I felt my body
      rising from the bed.
I rose slowly, slowly until I floated three or four feet above the
      floor.
Then, with a kind of swimming motion, I propelled myself toward
      the window.
Outside, I rose higher and higher, above the pasture, fence,
      above the clothesline, above the dark, haunted trees
      beyond the pasture.
And, all the time, I heard the music of flutes.
It seemed the wind made this music.
And sometimes there were voices singing.
All of this was a long time ago and I cannot remember the words
      the voices sang.
But I know I flew when I heard them.

9

I Dream
David Ignatow

I dream I am lying in the mud on my back and staring up into the sky. Which do I prefer, since I have the power to fly into the blue slate of air? It is summer. I decide quickly that by flying face up I have a view of the sky I could not get by flying in it, while I'd be missing the mud.

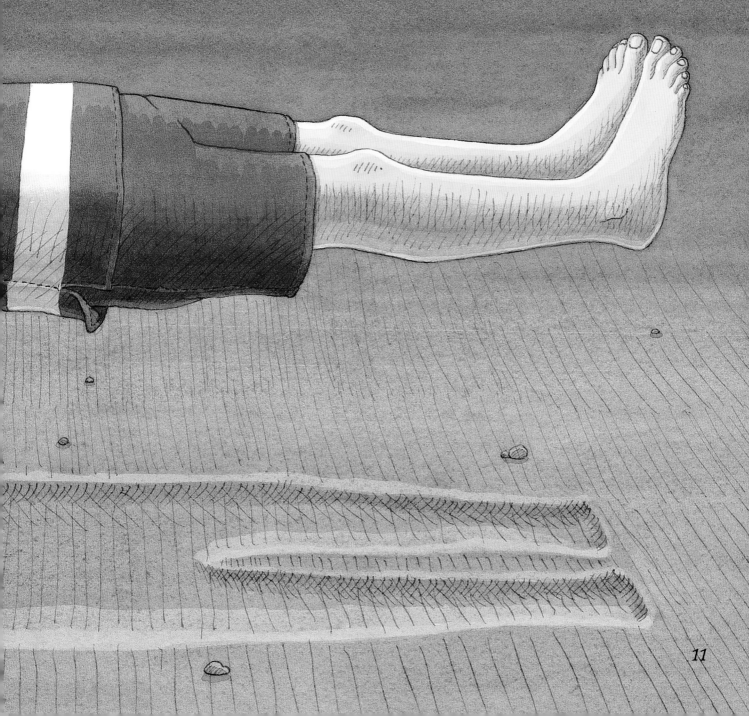

11

Flying-man
Mother Goose

Flying-man, Flying-man
Up in the sky,
Where are you going to,
Flying so high?

> *Over the mountains*
> *And over the sea—*

Flying-man, Flying-man
Can't you take me?

Big Dreams
April Halprin Wayland

The scruffy house cat
aches to fly—
she dreams all day of
wings and sky!

So tonight
she climbs the ladder,
mounts a platform,
nothing matters

except to catch
a thin trapeze
then hold on tight
with grace and ease.

She swings herself
by both front paws
then somersaults
to wild applause

of kitchen mice,
who, though dizzy,
encourage Cat,
to keep her busy.

Circus

Felice Holman

Sawdust is the earth
    and from it spring
    great poles that hold
    a canvas sky
        and in it fly
        bright, whirling stars,
        wheeling and spinning
        while a moon sweeps by.
Leap from that earth, would I,
Open my arms, take wing,
Soar in that sky, would I,
Out where calliopes sing.

16

17

If I Had the Power of Wings
Lillian M. Fisher

If I had the power of wings
      I would ride with an eagle
          fly with a hawk
             glide with a gull.

I would skim the highest mountain
      span the widest desert
          cross the boundless ocean.

In twilight, at dawn,
      in calm and in storm,
          my wings would brush you,
             my wings would touch you.

Together we would soar . . .

      if I had the power of wings.

The Wings of Song
Leslie Danford Perkins

I ride on wings of my song,
soaring upward to a height
I can reach only by singing.

Another voice joins mine
and the wings beat harder,
carrying me to a breathless height
I can never reach alone.

A hundred voices sing,
wings grow stronger,
strong enough to lift a hundred people
to a joyous height we can reach only
when we ride on the wings of our song.

20

For Poets
Al Young

Stay beautiful
but don't stay down underground too long
Don't turn into a mole
or a worm
or a root
or a stone

Come on out into the sunlight
Breathe in trees
Knock out mountains
Commune with snakes
& be the very hero of birds

Don't forget to poke your head up
& blink
think
Walk all around
Swim upstream

Don't forget to fly

Fairies
Langston Hughes

Out of the dust of dreams
Fairies weave their garments.
Out of the purple and rose of old memories
They make rainbow wings.
No wonder we find them such marvellous things!

Postscript
From The Cave of Nakedness
W. H. Auden

Since he weighs nothing,
Even the stoutest dreamer
Can fly without wings.

The Wing Box
Lee Bennett Hopkins

It's time
to take
them off.

Open the
Wing Box.

Tuck them in
wistfully—

DO NOT FOLD
DO NOT BEND
DO NOT CRUSH.

Lay them
calmly
quietly
hushed
for
tonight.

Close the lid
gently.

*Ready
for
tomorrow's
flight.*

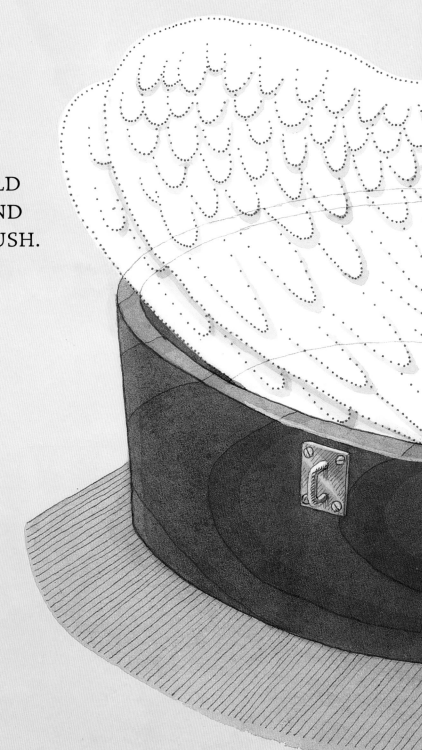

About the Poets

W. H. AUDEN, born in York, England, came to the United States in 1939. In 1948 he received the Pulitzer Prize for Poetry. In addition to a wide variety of writing, he created more than four hundred poems.

REBECCA KAI DOTLICH, author of several books of poetry, lives and works in Carmel, Indiana. Her works have been featured on *Reading Rainbow* as well as in many anthologies.

LILLIAN M. FISHER lives in Alpine, California, where she enjoys exploring her desert environment. She has spent a great deal of time on reservations studying Southwest Indian life.

FELICE HOLMAN is the author of numerous books of verse and the acclaimed novel *Slake's Limbo*. She lives in California.

LEE BENNETT HOPKINS lives in Cape Coral, Florida. His autobiographical *Been to Yesterdays: Poems of a Life* received many awards, including the Christopher Medal. In 2009 he received the National Council of Teachers of English Excellence in Poetry for Children Award for his aggregate body of work.

LANGSTON HUGHES is one of America's greatest poets. His classic book *The Dream Keeper and Other Poems*, published in 1932, has never been out of print.

DAVID IGNATOW was born in Brooklyn, New York. He created numerous volumes of adult poems as well as served as president of the Poetry Society of America.

ALDEN NOWLAN, one of Canada's most popular twentieth-century poets, was born in Stanley, Nova Scotia. The Alden Nowlan House at the University of New Brunswick is named in his honor.

LESLIE DANFORD PERKINS lives in California. Her poetry for children has appeared in many anthologies.

PRINCE REDCLOUD has penned numerous poems for children that have appeared in many anthologies, including *My America*, edited by Lee Bennett Hopkins.

APRIL HALPRIN WAYLAND is a poet, writer, and teacher who lives in California. Her verse novel *Girl Coming in for a Landing* received the Myra Cohn Livingston Award for Poetry and was named a Lee Bennett Hopkins Poetry Honor Book. Dozens of her poems have appeared in *Cricket* magazine.

AL YOUNG was named Poet Laureate of California in 2005. He was born in Ocean Springs, Mississippi, and his work has been translated into numerous languages. He twice received the American Book Award.

To Charles J. Egita, who encourages
everyone to soar ahead
—L. B. H.

To AnnaLi and Jack for sharing their
trampoline with me
—P. G.

Every effort has been made to locate all rights holders and to clear reprint permissions. If oversights have been made, we sincerely apologize and will be pleased to rectify the situation in future editions.

Thanks are due to the following for permission to reprint the works listed below:

Clarke, Irwin and Company, Ltd. for "I, Icarus" from *Bread, Wine, and Salt*. Copyright © 1967 by Alden Nowlan.

Curtis Brown Ltd. for "Wake Up, Wings!" by Rebecca Kai Dotlich, copyright © 2010 by Rebecca Kai Dotlich; "The Wing Box" by Lee Bennett Hopkins, copyright © 2010 by Lee Bennett Hopkins; "Of Wings" by Prince Redcloud, copyright © 1992 by Prince Redcloud, first appeared in *To the Zoo: Animal Poems*, published by Little, Brown & Co. All reprinted by permission of Curtis Brown Ltd.

Lillian M. Fisher for "If I Had the Power of Wings." Copyright © 2010 by Lillian M. Fisher. Used by permission of the author, who controls all rights.

Felice Holman for "Circus" from *The Song in My Head* (Charles Scribner's Sons, Copyright © 1985 by Felice Holman). Used by permission of the author, who controls all rights.

Leslie Danford Perkins for "The Wings of Song." Copyright © 2010 by Leslie Danford Perkins. Used by permission of the author, who controls all rights.

Random House, Inc., for "The Cave of Nakedness: Postscript" from *Collected Poems* by W. H. Auden, copyright © 1963 by W. H. Auden, used by permission of Random House, Inc.; "Fairies" from *The Collected Poems of Langston Hughes* by Langston Hughes, copyright © 1994, by the Estate of Langston Hughes, used by permission of Alfred A. Knopf, a division of Random House, Inc.

April Halprin Wayland for "Big Dreams." Copyright © 2010 by April Halprin Wayland. Used by permission of the author, who controls all rights.

Wesleyan University Press for "I Dream" from *New and Collected Poems, 1970-1985*, copyright © 1986 by David Ignatow. Reprinted by permission of Wesleyan University Press.

Al Young for "For Poets." Copyright © 1971, 1992 by Al Young. Used by permission of the author, who controls all rights.

Compilation copyright © 2010 by Lee Bennett Hopkins
Illustrations copyright © 2010 by Ponder Goembel
All Rights Reserved
HOLIDAY HOUSE is registered in the U.S. Patent and Trademark Office.
Printed and bound in April 2010 at Kwong Fat Offset Co., Ltd., Dongguan City,
Quang Dong Province, China.
The text typeface is Breughel.
The illustrations were done in colored ink line with acrylic wash.
www.holidayhouse.com
First Edition
1 3 5 7 9 10 8 6 4 2

Library of Congress Cataloging-in-Publication Data

Give me wings : poems / selected by Lee Bennett Hopkins ; illustrated by Ponder Goembel. — 1st ed.
p. cm.
ISBN 978-0-8234-2023-0 (hardcover)
1. Flight—Juvenile poetry. 2. Children's poetry, American.
I. Hopkins, Lee Bennett. II. Goembel, Ponder, ill.
PS595.F59G58 2010
811'.5080356—dc22
2009014744